JONATHAN CAPE

UK | USA | Canada | Ireland | Australia
India | New Zealand | South Africa

Jonathan Cape is part of the Penguin Random House group of companies
whose addresses can be found at global.penguinrandomhouse.com.

www.penguin.co.uk    www.puffin.co.uk    www.ladybird.co.uk

Penguin
Random House
UK

First published 2021
001

Printed in China
A CIP catalogue record for this book is available from the British Library

The authorized representative in the EEA is Penguin Random
House Ireland, Morrison Chambers, 32 Nassau Street, Dublin D02 YH68

ISBN: 978–0–857–55119–1

All correspondence to:
Jonathan Cape, Penguin Random House Children's
One Embassy Gardens, 8 Viaduct Gardens,
London SW11 7BW

# Stanley's
### Library

JONATHAN CAPE • LONDON

It's going to be another busy day
at Stanley's Library.

Charlie tidies the bookshelves
while Stanley puts all sorts of books
on to his trolley.

Next, he wheels the trolley
into the library van.

Stanley drives to the village green
and opens the van's big doors.

# The mobile library is ready for visitors!

First in the queue is Myrtle. She's returning
the five books all about cheese
she borrowed last week.

This week, she would like to borrow five MORE books - all about cheese, please!

Also on the village green are Benjamin, Sophie and Betty. Benjamin borrows a scary book.

Sophie borrows a scary, hairy book.
And Betty borrows a scary, hairy, fairy book!

Stanley spots Hattie oiling her motorbike.
He has a surprise for her that he knows
she will LOVE.

Thank you, Stanley!

Shamus has ordered a book
to help him with his rigging.

And Stanley has a book
for Little Woo, too.
Thank you, Stanley.

PIRATES!

LOTS OF
KNOTS

LATEST EDITION

Stanley gets back to the library in time
to help Charlie arrange all the chairs . . .

. . . for a special event!

Everyone has dressed in space costumes.
Well, almost everyone.

They all settle down to hear the famous author - Agatha Mouse - read from her new book.
Thank you, Agatha!

# Well! What a busy day!

Stanley's
House

Time for tea!
Time for a bath!

And time for bed!
Goodnight, Stanley.

# Stanley

If you liked **Stanley's Library** then you'll love these other books about Stanley:

Stanley the Builder

Stanley's Café

Stanley the Farmer

Stanley's Garage

Stanley the Postman

Stanley's Shop

Stanley's School

Stanley's Train

Stanley's Fire Engine

Stanley's Numbers

Stanley's Opposites

Stanley's Colours

Stanley's Shapes

Stanley's Paintbox

Stanley's Toolbox

Stanley's Lunch Box

Stanley's Toy Box

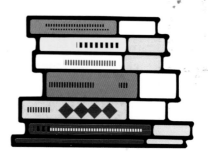